Welcome, Kind Reader, to a Tale of Asgard...

Thor, the prince of Asgard, is a brash and impetuous youth. Never one to consider who he is or what he has, Thor's mind is always on who he will one day be and what the future holds for him. He feels he lives in the shadow of his father, Odin, ruler of all Asgard, and he hopes he can escape that fate through noble deeds and valiant acts.

When Odin asks Thor and his fellow young warriors, Balder and Sif, to undertake a quest on his behalf, Thor quickly agrees, without consulting his friends. Together they travel Asgard in search of four mystic elements which Odin hopes to forge into an enchanted sword. Though danger meets them at almost every turn, the trio of young warriors is able to collect the first three objects. But on their way to retrieve the fourth, Thor's younger half-brother, Loki, appears and warns them that the evil Norn Queen, Karnilla, is planning to attack Asgard. Along with Sif and Balder, Loki returns to Asgard to alert Odin of the impending onslaught, while Thor continues on alone to obtain the final element: water from the mystical Lake of Lilitha. However, upon reaching the shores of the Lilitha, Thor discovers that the lake had been dried and his quest has failed. All he can bring back now is a handful of dirt from the arid lake bed.

Thor returns home to find Asgard under attack. Karnilla's monstrous army has laid siege to the city and threatens all Thor holds dear. Without hesitation, Thor joins Sif and Balder to defend Asgard against the forces of evil. The tide of battle turns, and the Asgardian warriors are able to drive the invading beasts back. But, just as victory is theirs, Thor is struck down by a magic arrow– the Son of Asgard is dead!

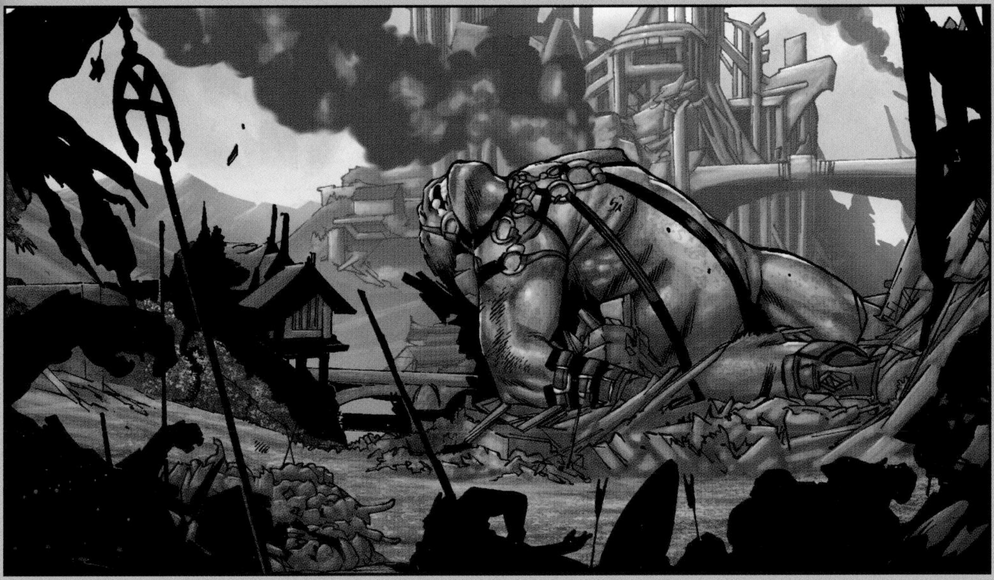

Part Six
The Trio Triumphant

Akira Yoshida
WRITER

Greg Tocchini
PENCILER

Jay Leisten
INKER

Guru eFX
COLORIST

VC's Randy Gentile
LETTERER

Adi Granov
COVER ARTIST

MacKenzie Cadenhead
EDITOR

Ralph Macchio & C.B. Cebulski
CONSULTING EDITORS

Joe Quesada
EDITOR IN CHIEF

Dan Buckley
PUBLISHER

MARVEL   Spotlight

VISIT US AT
www.abdopublishing.com

Reinforced library bound edition published in 2007 by Spotlight, a division of the ABDO Publishing Group, Edina, Minnesota. Spotlight produces high quality reinforced library bound editions for schools and libraries. Published by agreement with Marvel Characters, Inc.

Library of Congress Cataloging-in-Publication Data

Yoshida, Akira.
Thor, son of Asgard / [Akira Yoshida, writer ; Greg Tocchini, penciler ; Jay Leisten, inker ; Guru e FX, colorist ; Adi Granov, cover artist ; Randy Gentile, letterer].
p. cm.
Cover title.
"Marvel Age."
Revisions of issues 1-6 of the serial Thor, son of Asgard.
Contents: pt. 1. The warriors teen -- pt. 2. The heat of Hakurei -- pt. 3. The nest of Gnori -- pt. 4. The jaws of Jennia -- pt. 5. The lake of Lilitha -- pt. 6. The trio triumphant.
ISBN-13: 978-1-59961-286-7 (pt. 1)
ISBN-10: 1-59961-286-0 (pt. 1)
ISBN-13: 978-1-59961-287-4 (pt. 2)
ISBN-10: 1-59961-287-9 (pt. 2)
ISBN-13: 978-1-59961-288-1 (pt. 3)
ISBN-10: 1-59961-288-7 (pt. 3)
ISBN-13: 978-1-59961-289-8 (pt. 4)
ISBN-10: 1-59961-289-5 (pt. 4)
ISBN-13: 978-1-59961-290-4 (pt. 5)
ISBN-10: 1-59961-290-9 (pt. 5)
ISBN-13: 978-1-59961-291-1 (pt. 6)
ISBN-10: 1-59961-291-7 (pt. 6)
1. Comic books, strips, etc. I. Tocchini, Greg. II. Title. III. Title: Warriors teen. IV. Title: Heat of Hakurei. V. Title: Nest of Gnori. VI. Title: Jaws of Jennia. VII. Title: Lake of Lilitha. VIII. Title: Trio triumphant.

PN6728.T64Y68 2007
791.5'73--dc22

2006050635

Spotlight

All Spotlight books are reinforced library binding
and manufactured in the United States of America.

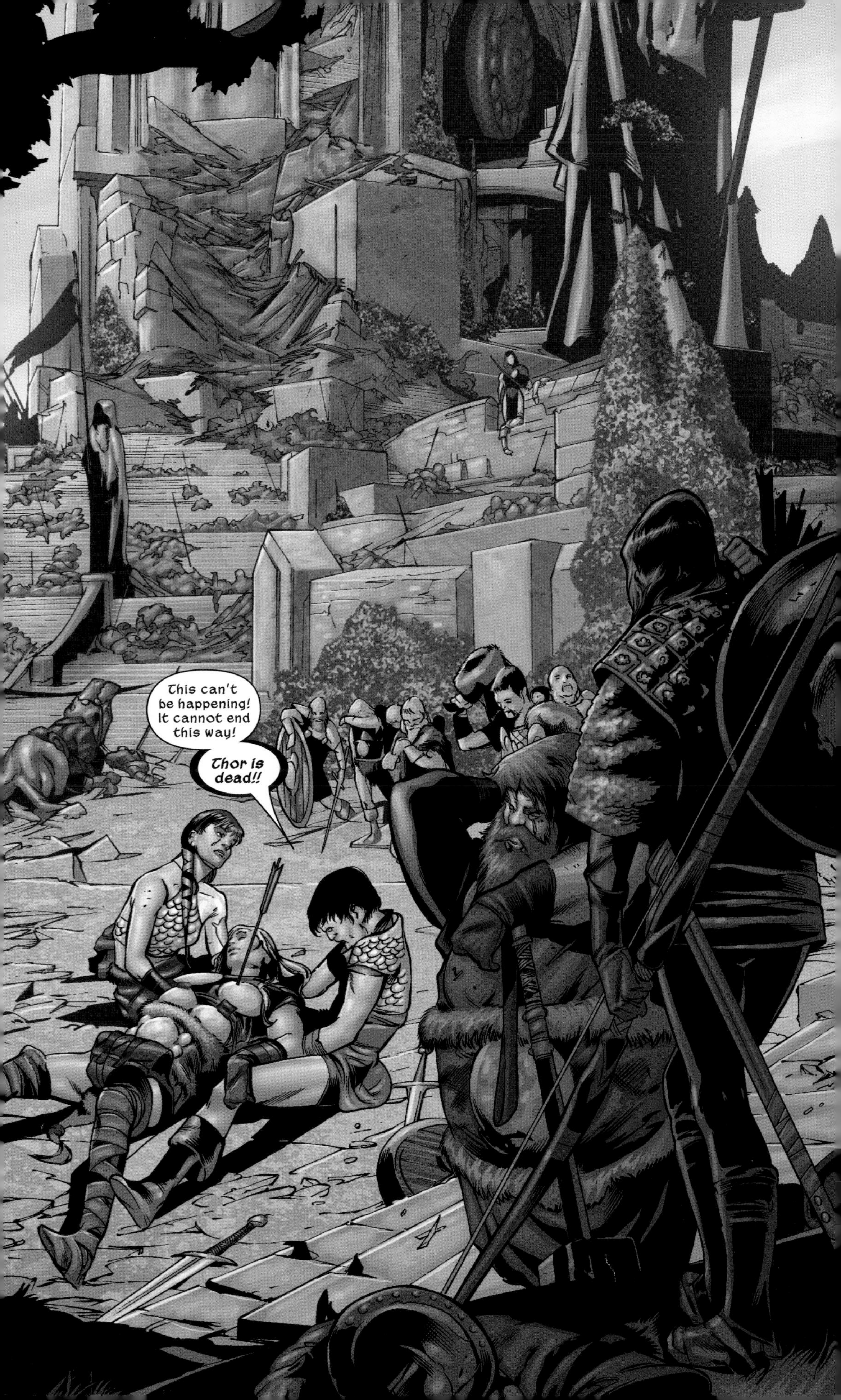
This can't be happening! It cannot end this way!
Thor is dead!!

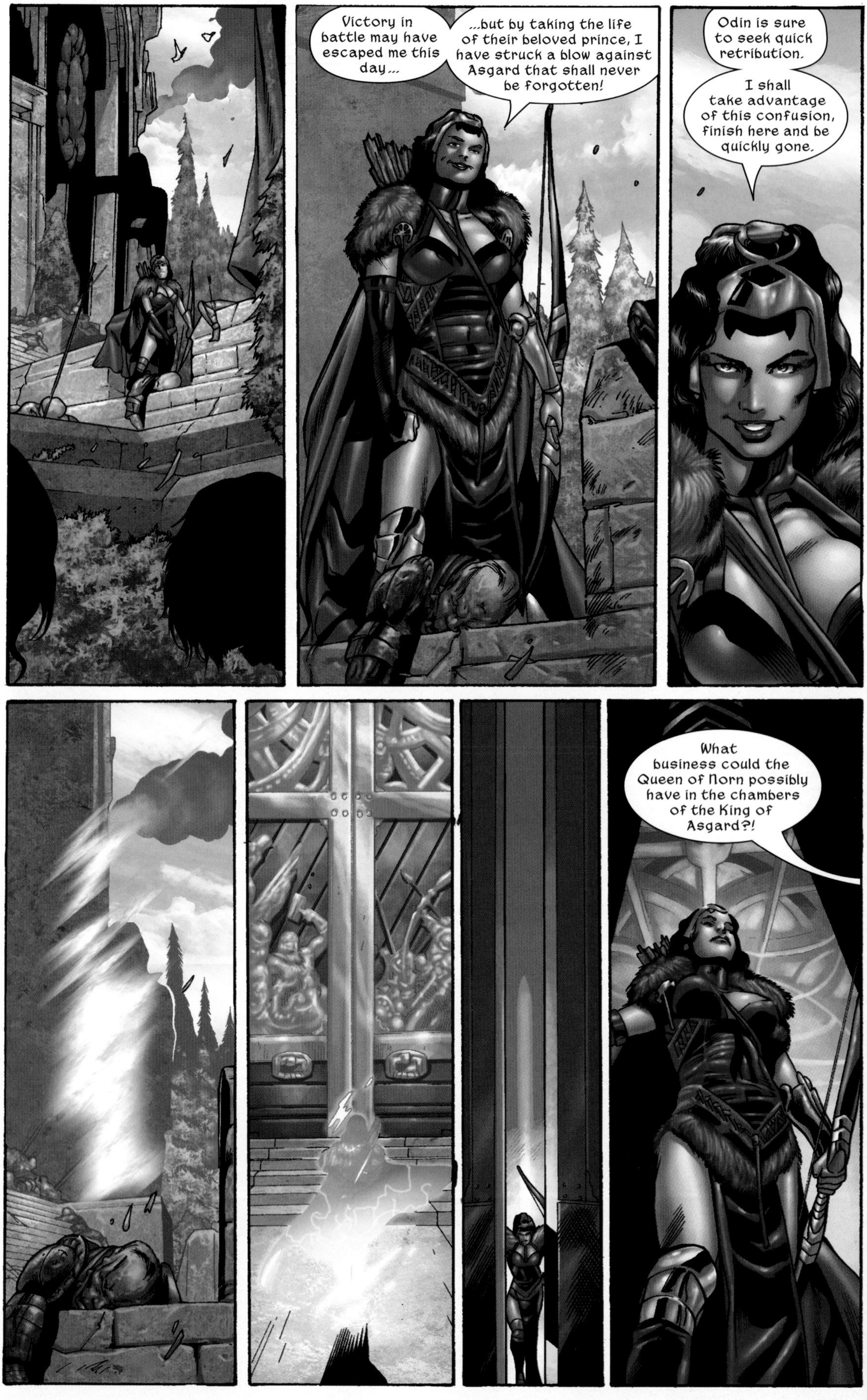
Victory in battle may have escaped me this day...
...but by taking the life of their beloved prince, I have struck a blow against Asgard that shall never be forgotten!
Odin is sure to seek quick retribution.
I shall take advantage of this confusion, finish here and be quickly gone.
What business could the Queen of Norn possibly have in the chambers of the King of Asgard?!

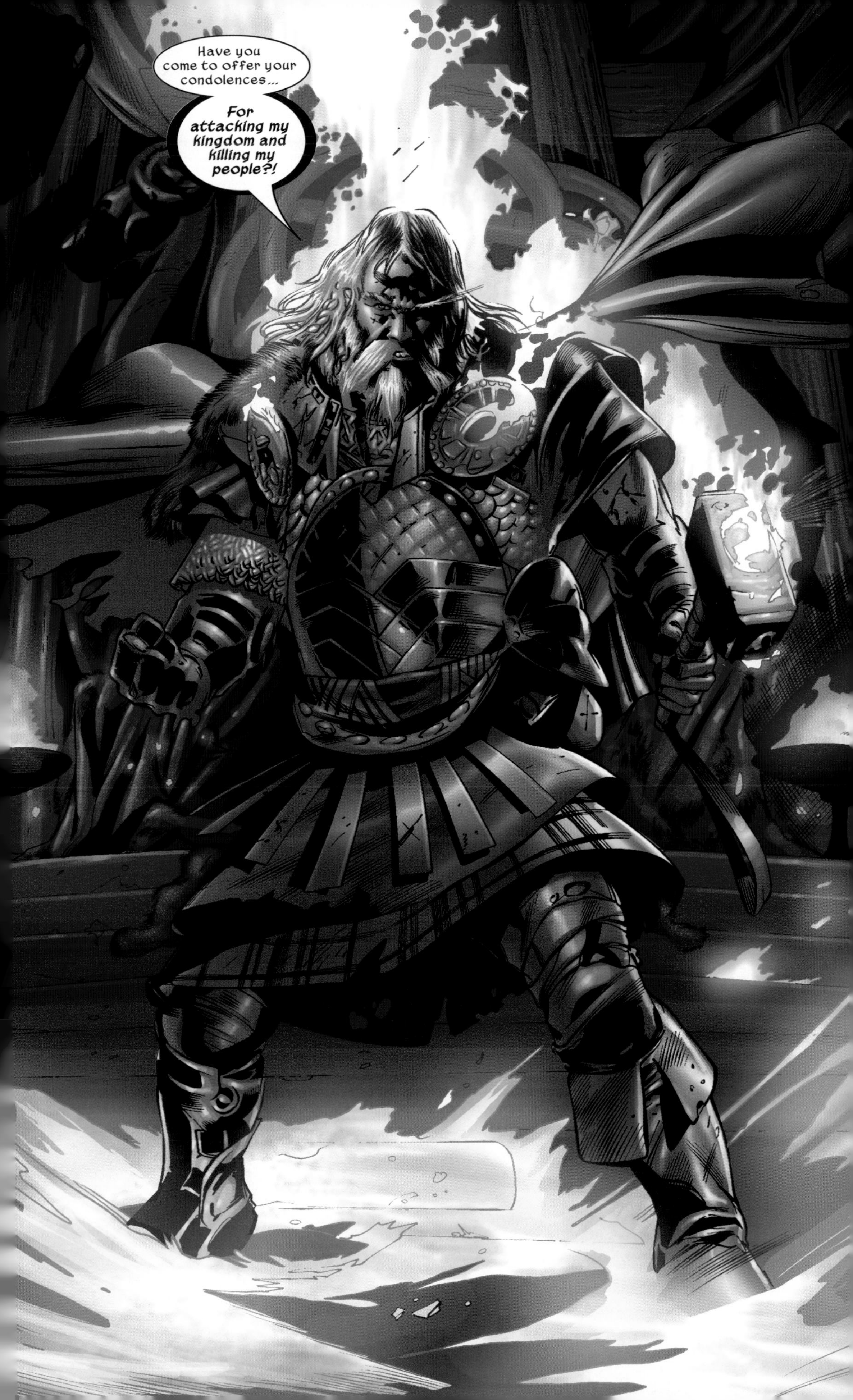
Have you come to offer your condolences...
For attacking my kingdom and killing my people?!

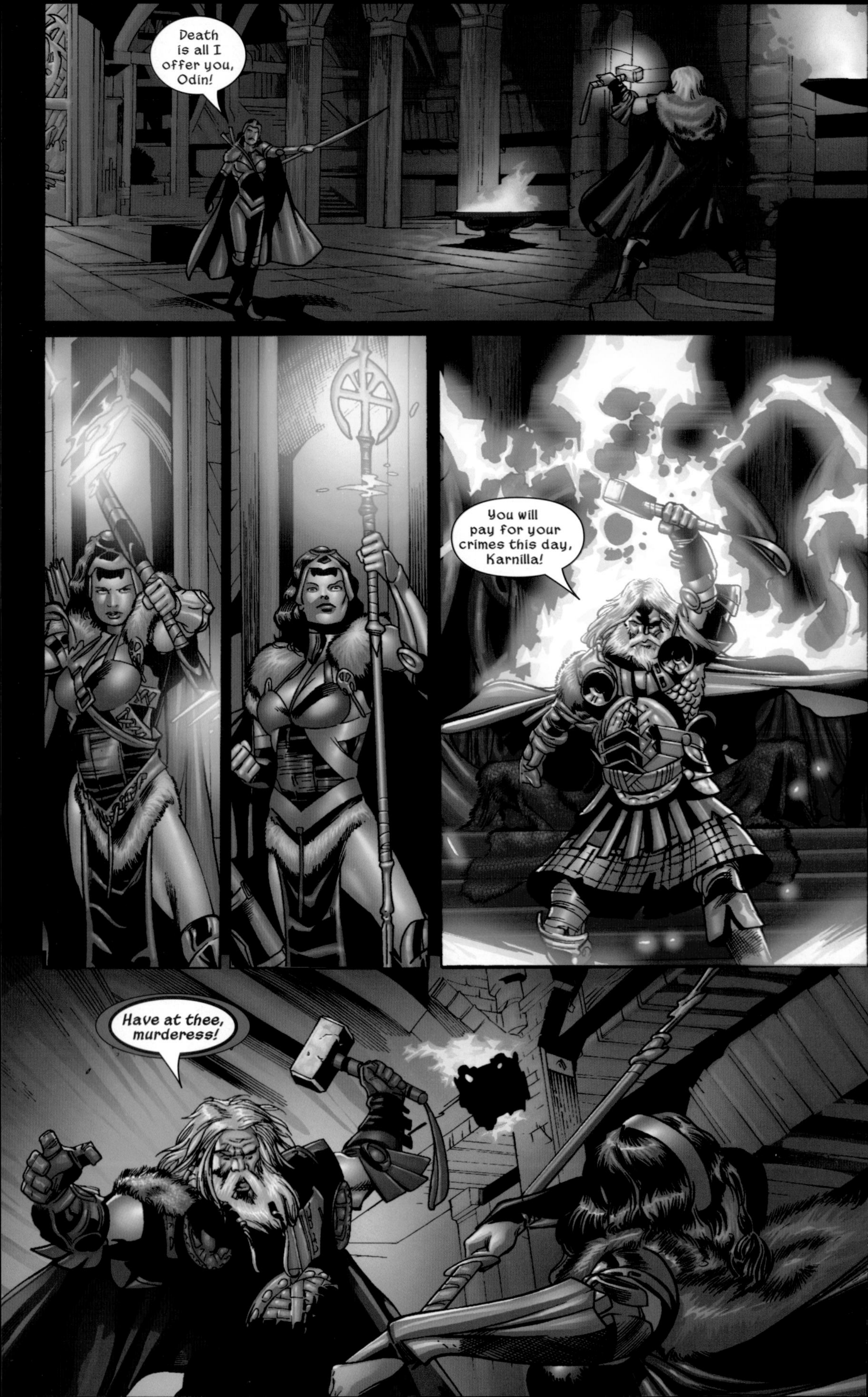
Death is all I offer you, Odin!
You will pay for your crimes this day, Karnilla!
Have at thee, murderess!

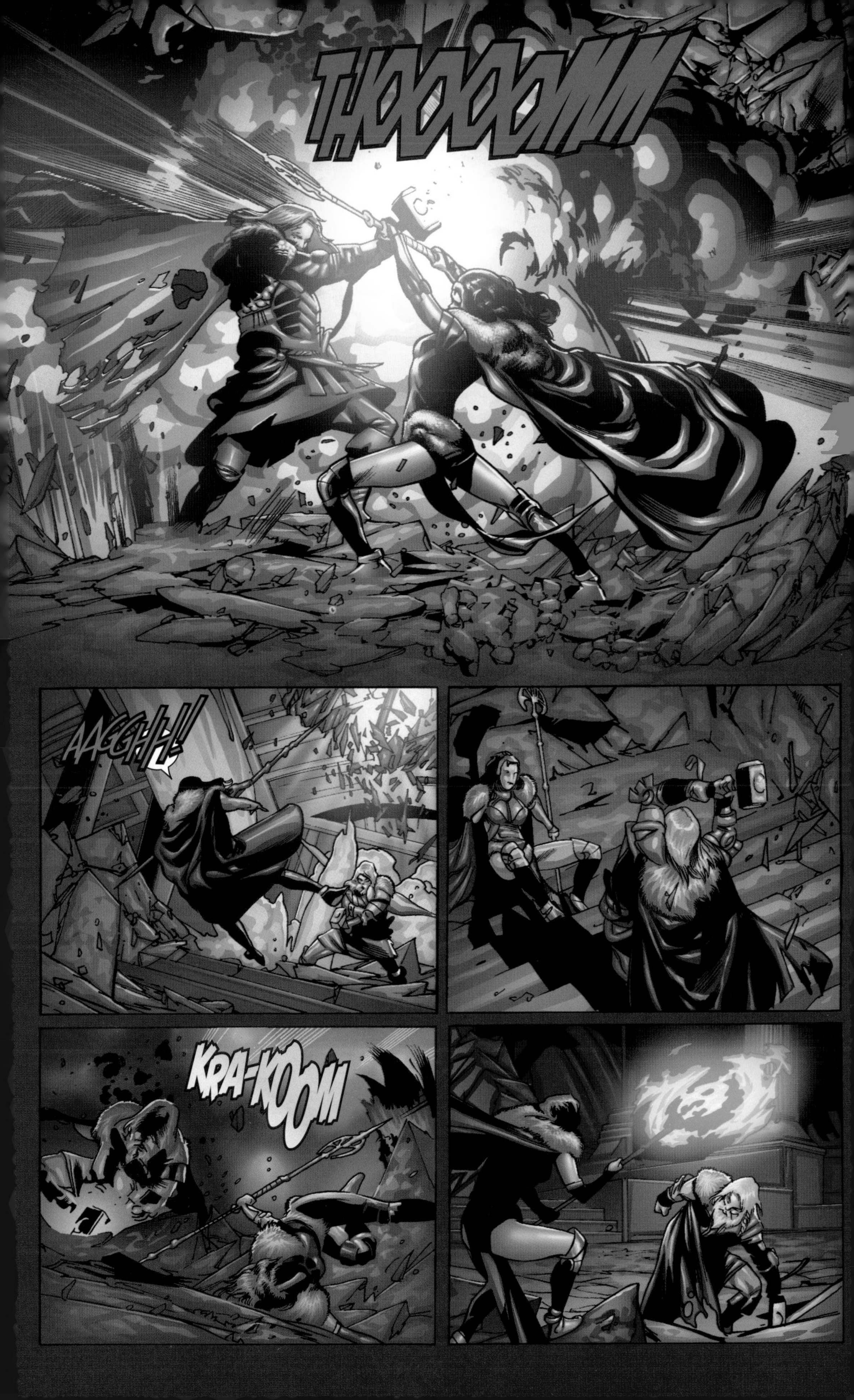
THOOOOOMM
AAGGHH!!
KRA-KOOM

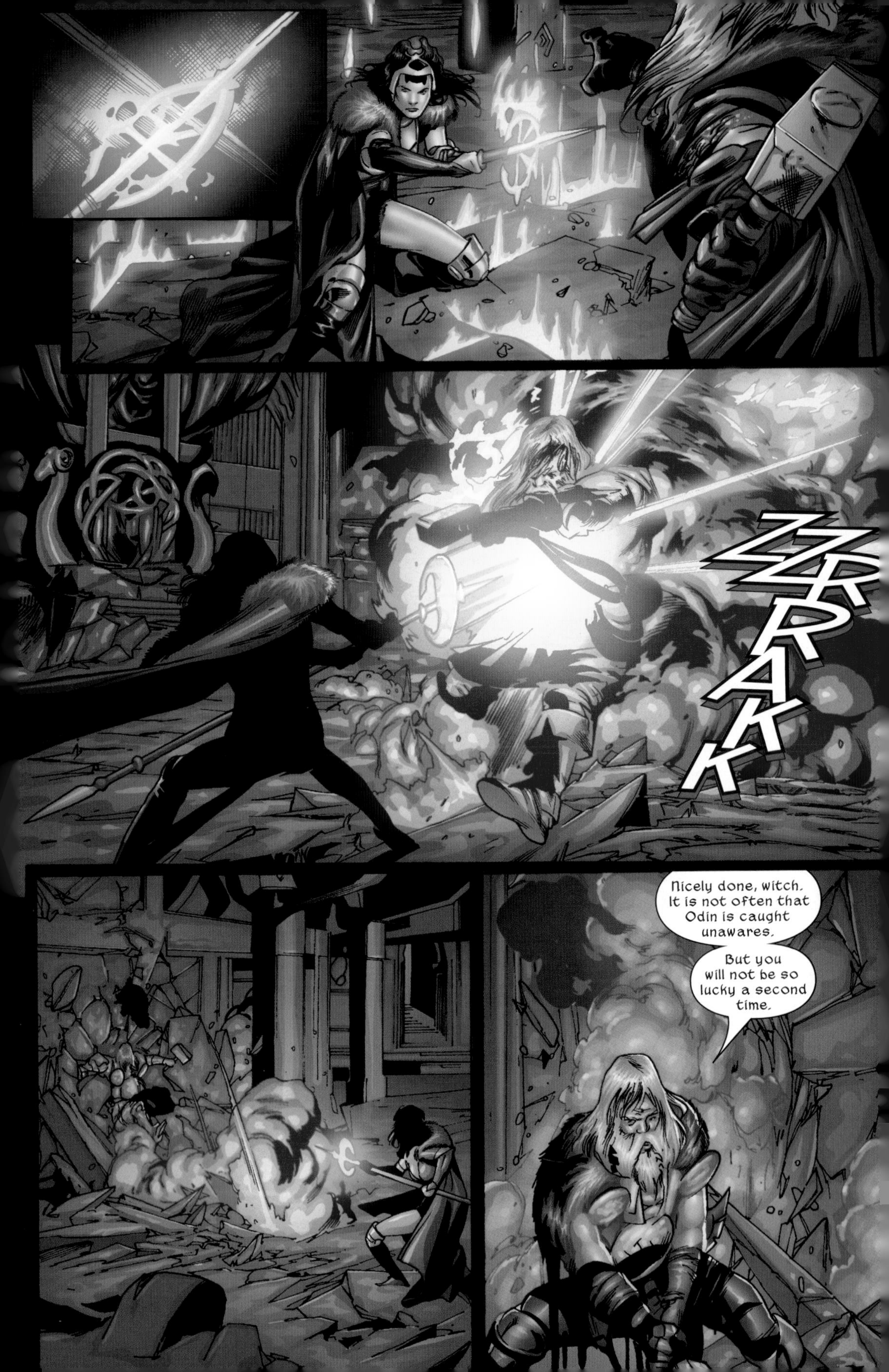
ZZRRAKK
Nicely done, witch. It is not often that Odin is caught unawares.
But you will not be so lucky a second time.

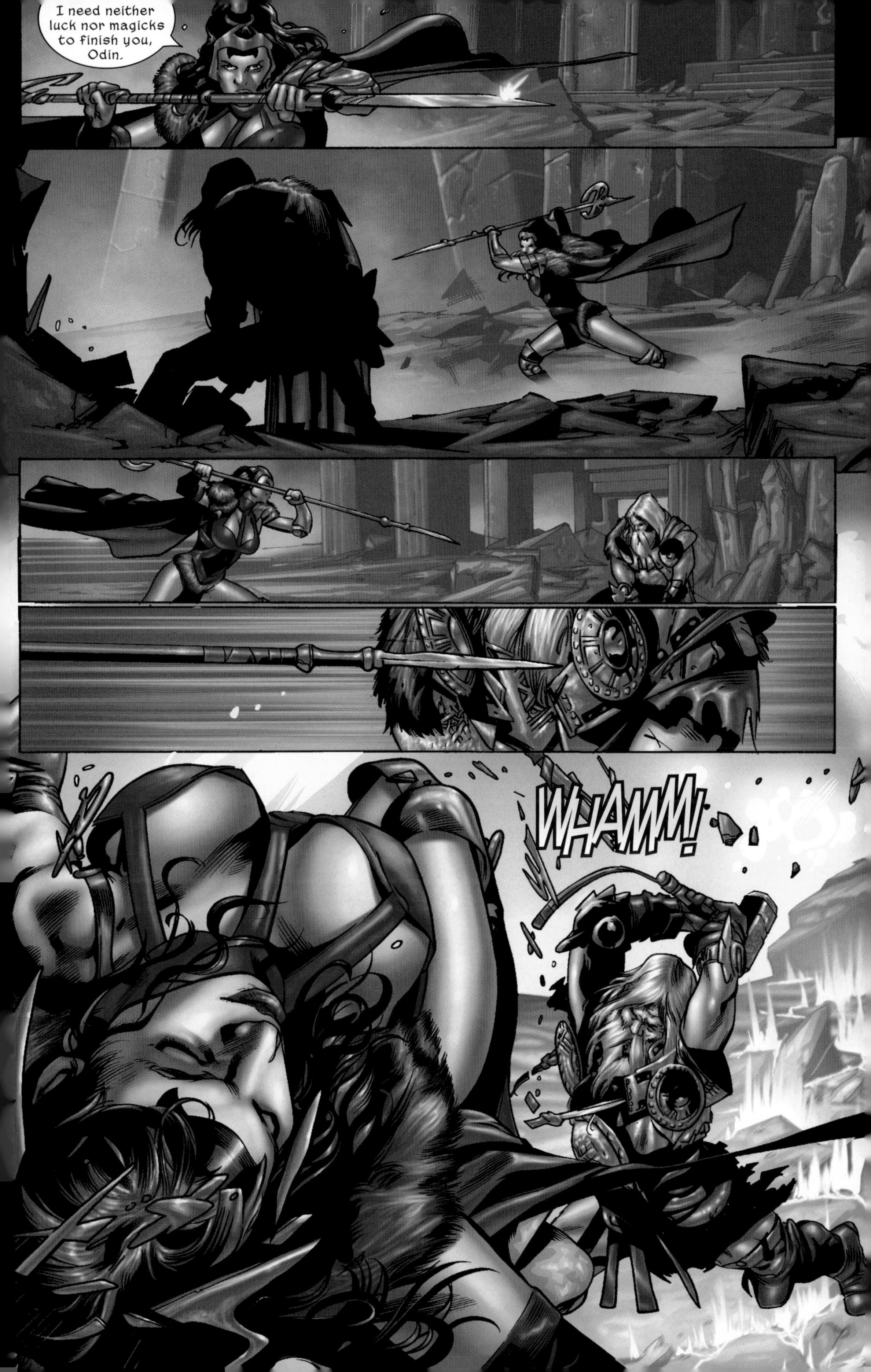
I need neither luck nor magicks to finish you, Odin.
WHAMM!

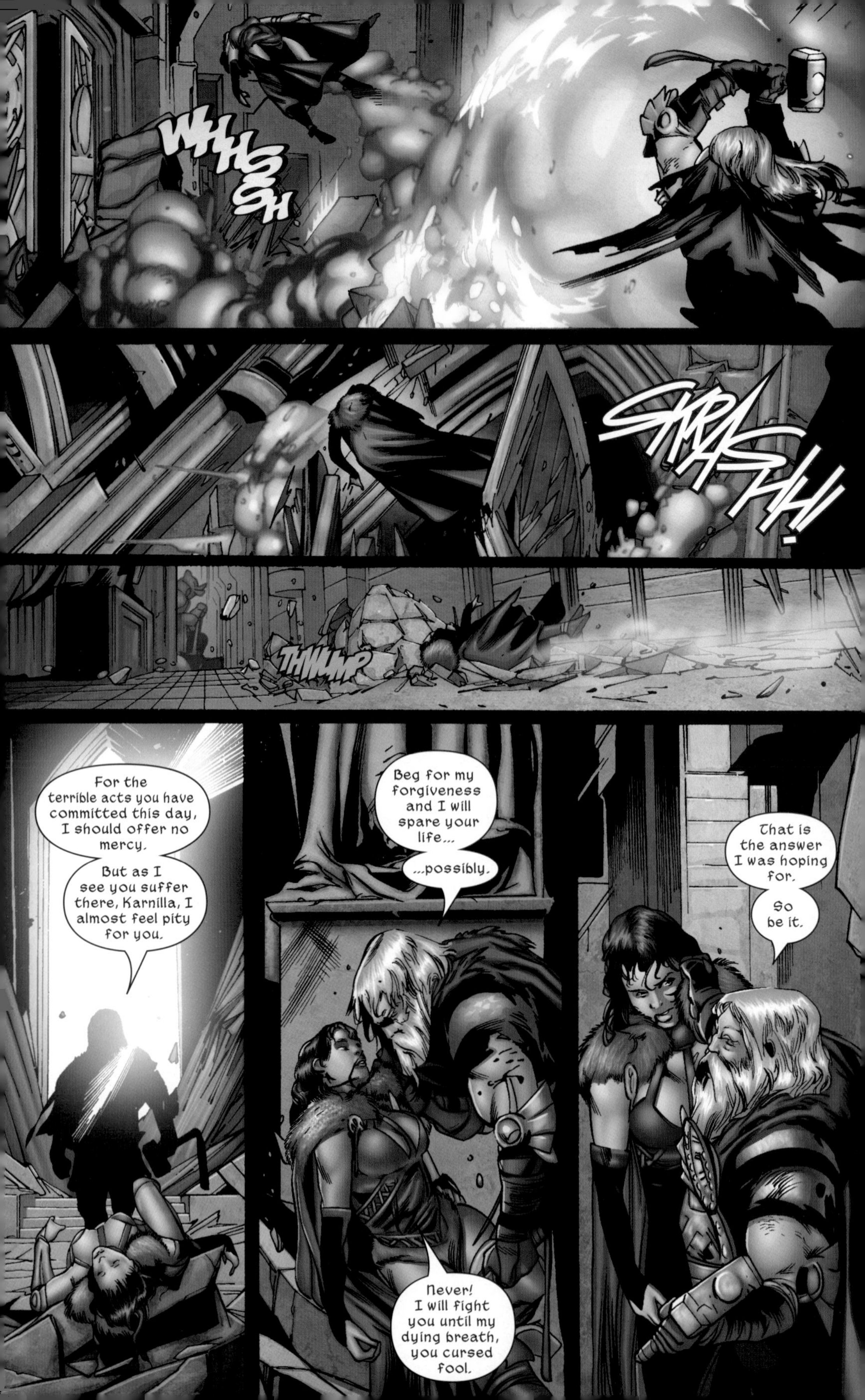
WHOOSH
SKRASHH!!
THWUMP
For the terrible acts you have committed this day, I should offer no mercy.
But as I see you suffer there, Karnilla, I almost feel pity for you.
Beg for my forgiveness and I will spare your life...
...possibly.
Never! I will fight you until my dying breath, you cursed fool.
That is the answer I was hoping for.
So be it.

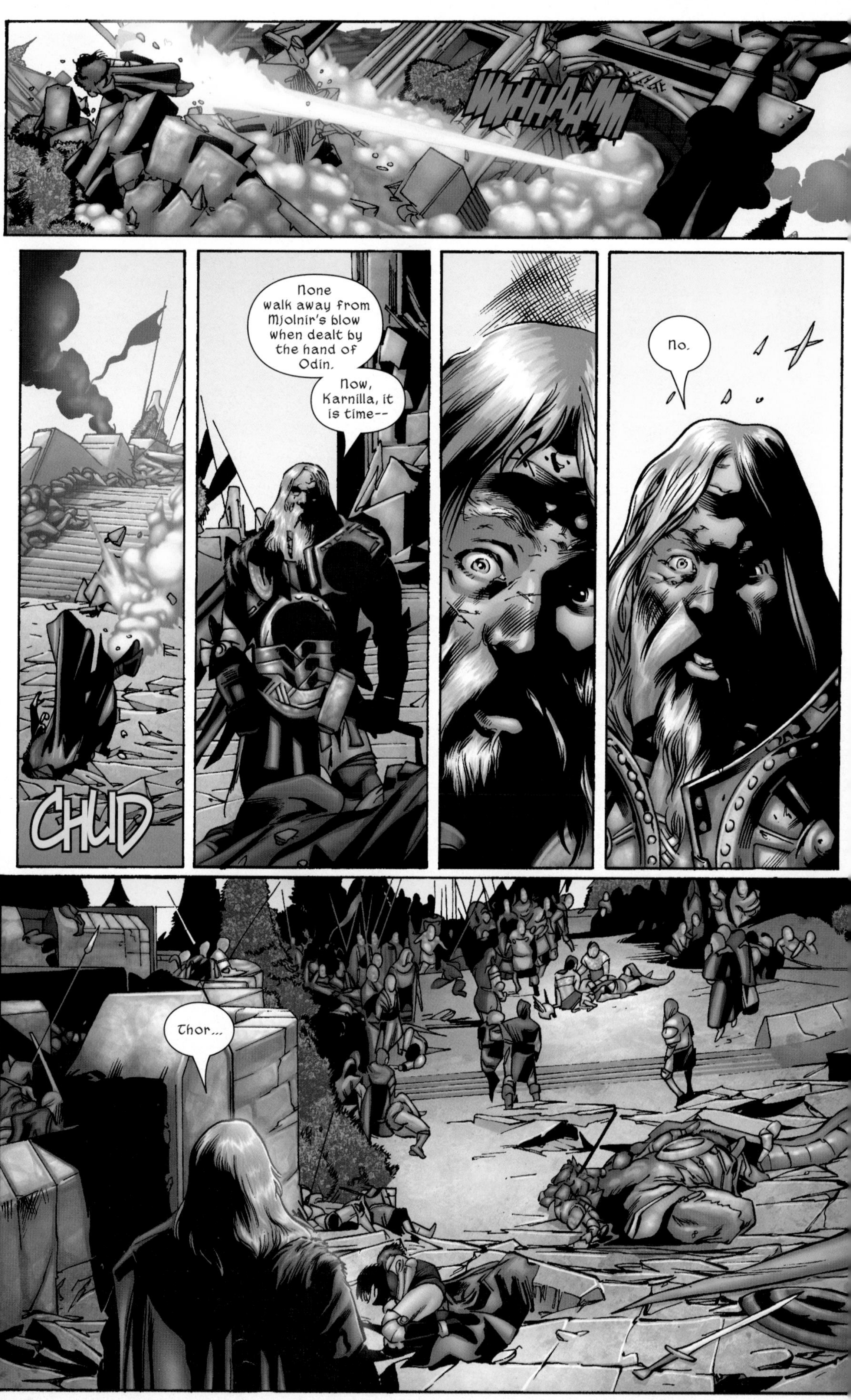
WHHAAMM
CHUD
None walk away from Mjolnir's blow when dealt by the hand of Odin.
Now, Karnilla, it is time--
No.
Thor...

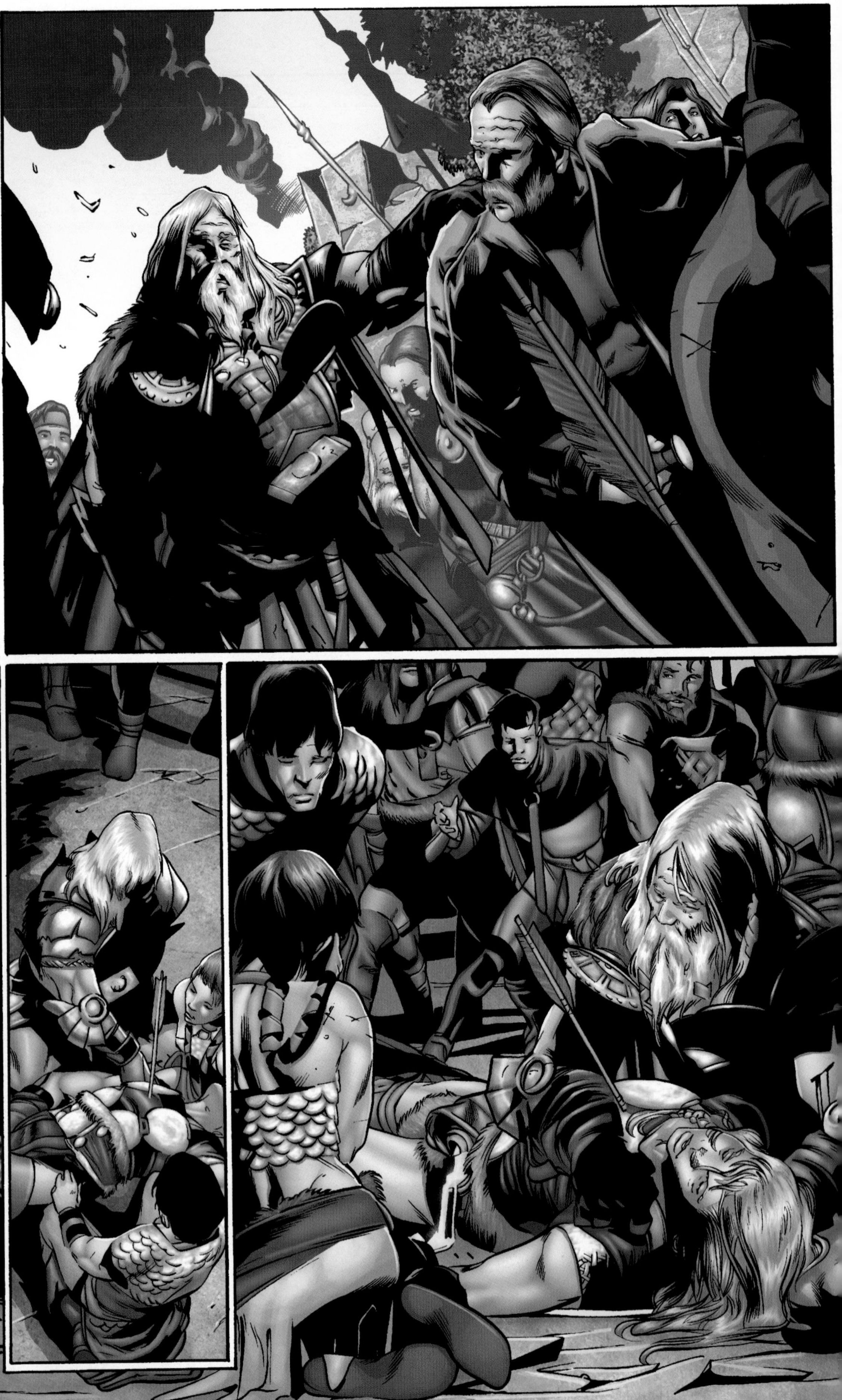

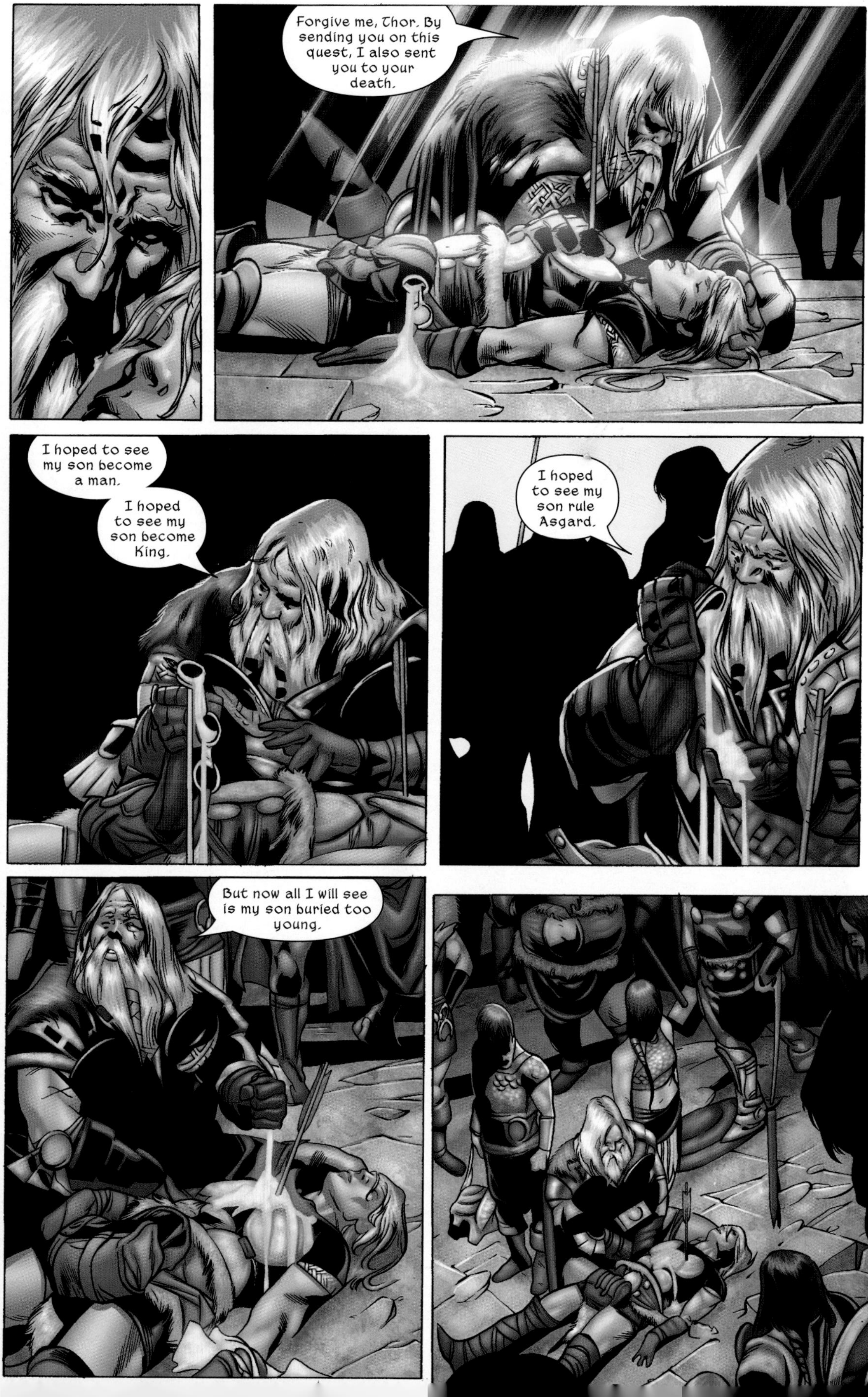
Forgive me, Thor. By sending you on this quest, I also sent you to your death.
I hoped to see my son become a man.
I hoped to see my son become King.
I hoped to see my son rule Asgard.
But now all I will see is my son buried too young.

My Lord, there are no words to describe the breaking of a heart... but ours have been shattered by the tragedy this day.

Asgard will mourn Thor's passing. He was beloved by all.

Most of all by you both.

A father's love for his son is expected... often taken for granted.

A friend's love, however, must be earned and given freely.

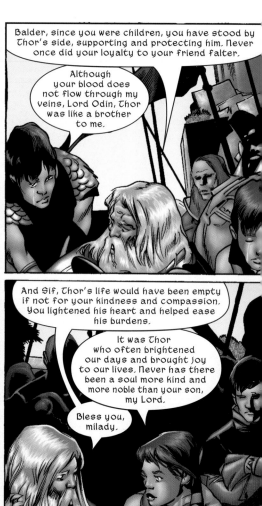

Balder, since you were children, you have stood by Thor's side, supporting and protecting him. Never once did your loyalty to your friend falter.

Although your blood does not flow through my veins, Lord Odin, Thor was like a brother to me.

And Sif, Thor's life would have been empty if not for your kindness and compassion. You lightened his heart and helped ease his burdens.

It was Thor who often brightened our days and brought joy to our lives. Never has there been a soul more kind and more noble than your son, my Lord.

Bless you, milady.

I lost my son... but you lost a friend.

The pain and suffering shall be ours to bear...

...but ours to share.

Farewell...

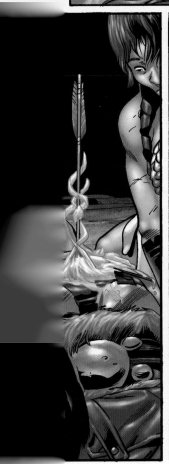

What's happening here?!

The dirt turns to water?

The waters of the Lake of Lilitha....

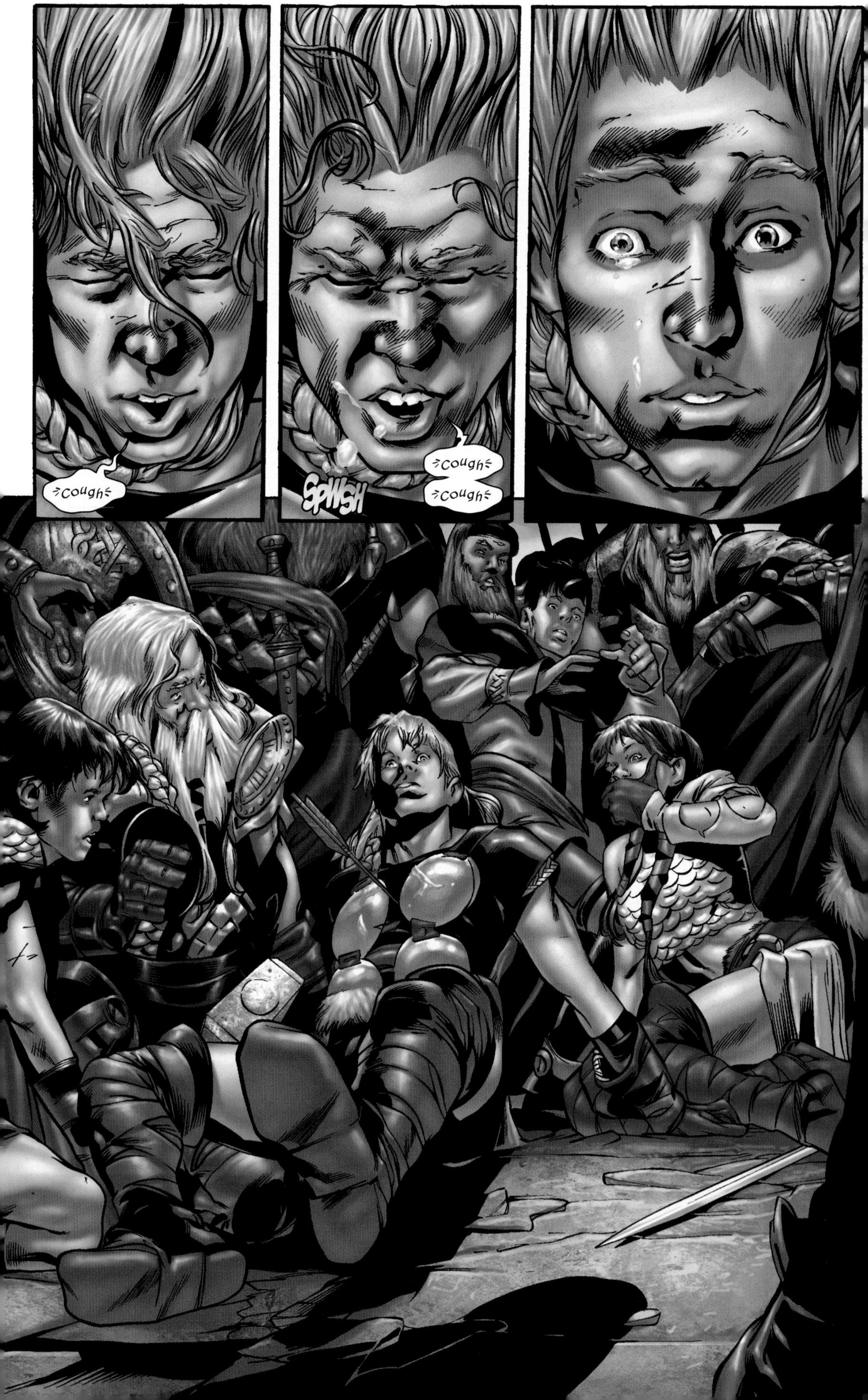
Cough
SPWSH
Cough
Cough

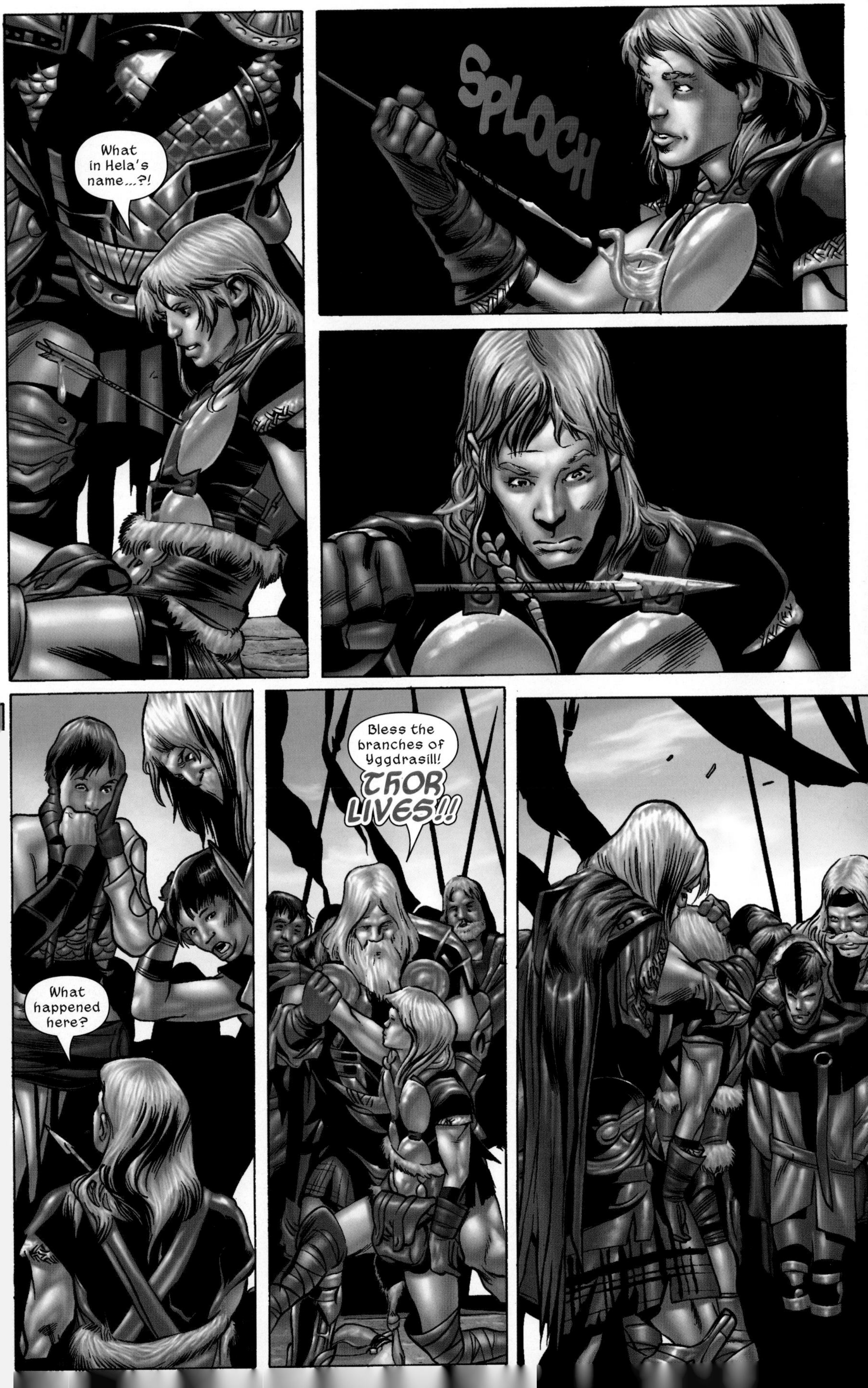

What in Hela's name...?!
SPLOCH
What happened here?
Bless the branches of Yggdrasill! THOR LIVES!!!

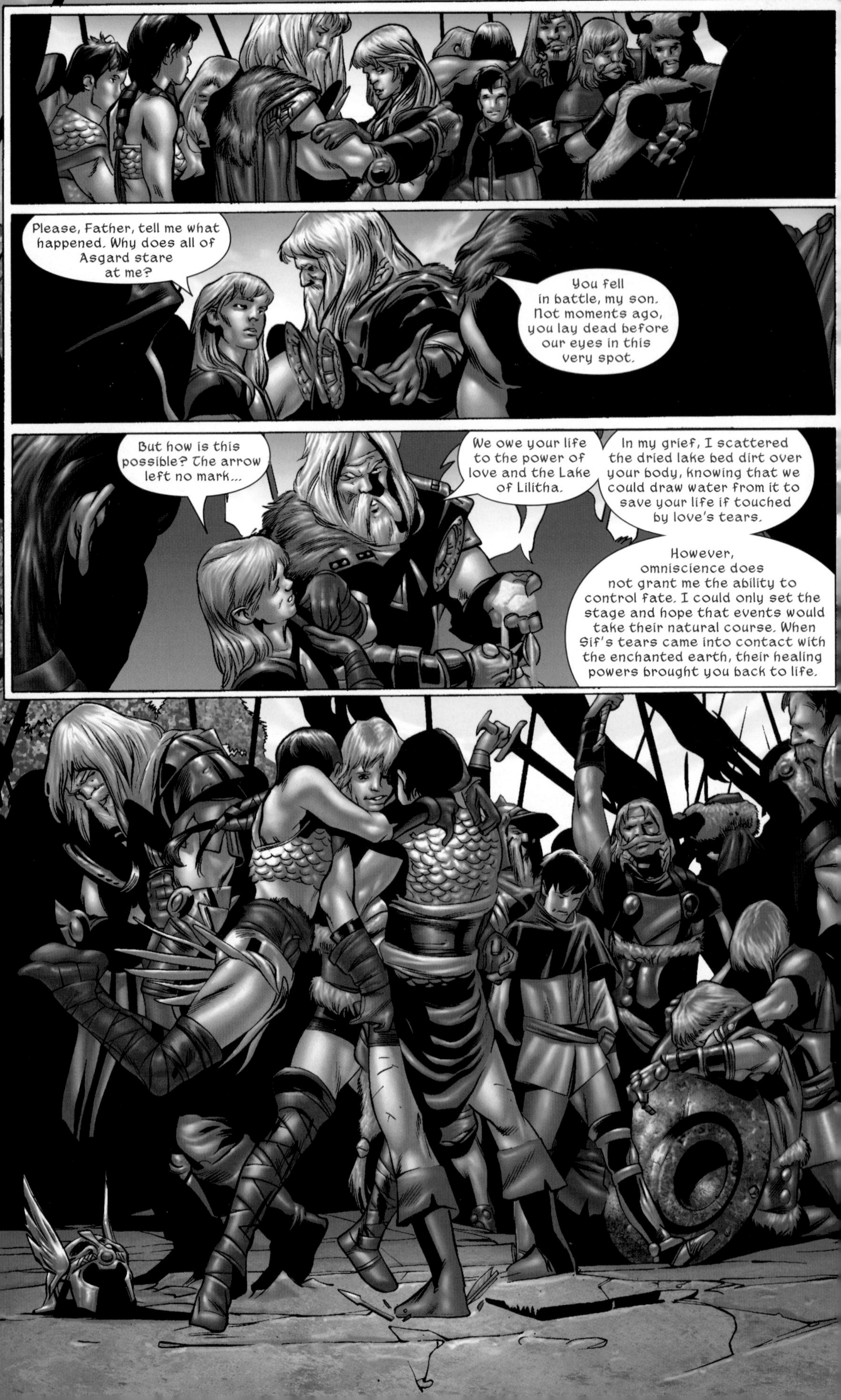
Please, Father, tell me what happened. Why does all of Asgard stare at me?
You fell in battle, my son. Not moments ago, you lay dead before our eyes in this very spot.
But how is this possible? The arrow left no mark...
We owe your life to the power of love and the Lake of Lilitha.
In my grief, I scattered the dried lake bed dirt over your body, knowing that we could draw water from it to save your life if touched by love's tears.
However, omniscience does not grant me the ability to control fate. I could only set the stage and hope that events would take their natural course. When Sif's tears came into contact with the enchanted earth, their healing powers brought you back to life.

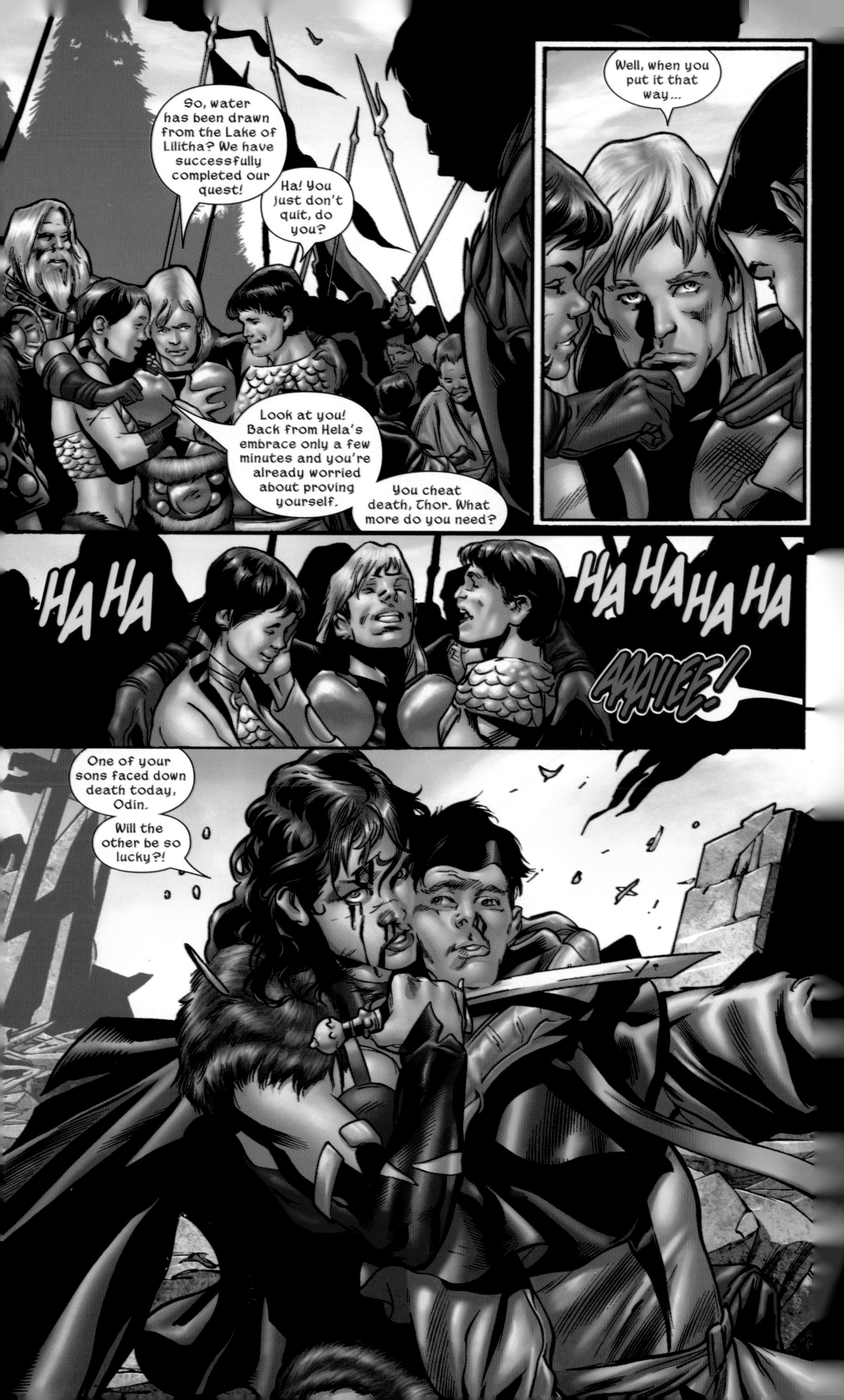
So, water has been drawn from the Lake of Lilitha? We have successfully completed our quest!
Ha! You just don't quit, do you?
Look at you! Back from Hela's embrace only a few minutes and you're already worried about proving yourself.
You cheat death, Thor. What more do you need?
Well, when you put it that way...
HA HA HA
HA HA HA HA HA HA
AAAIIEE!
One of your sons faced down death today, Odin.
Will the other be so lucky?!

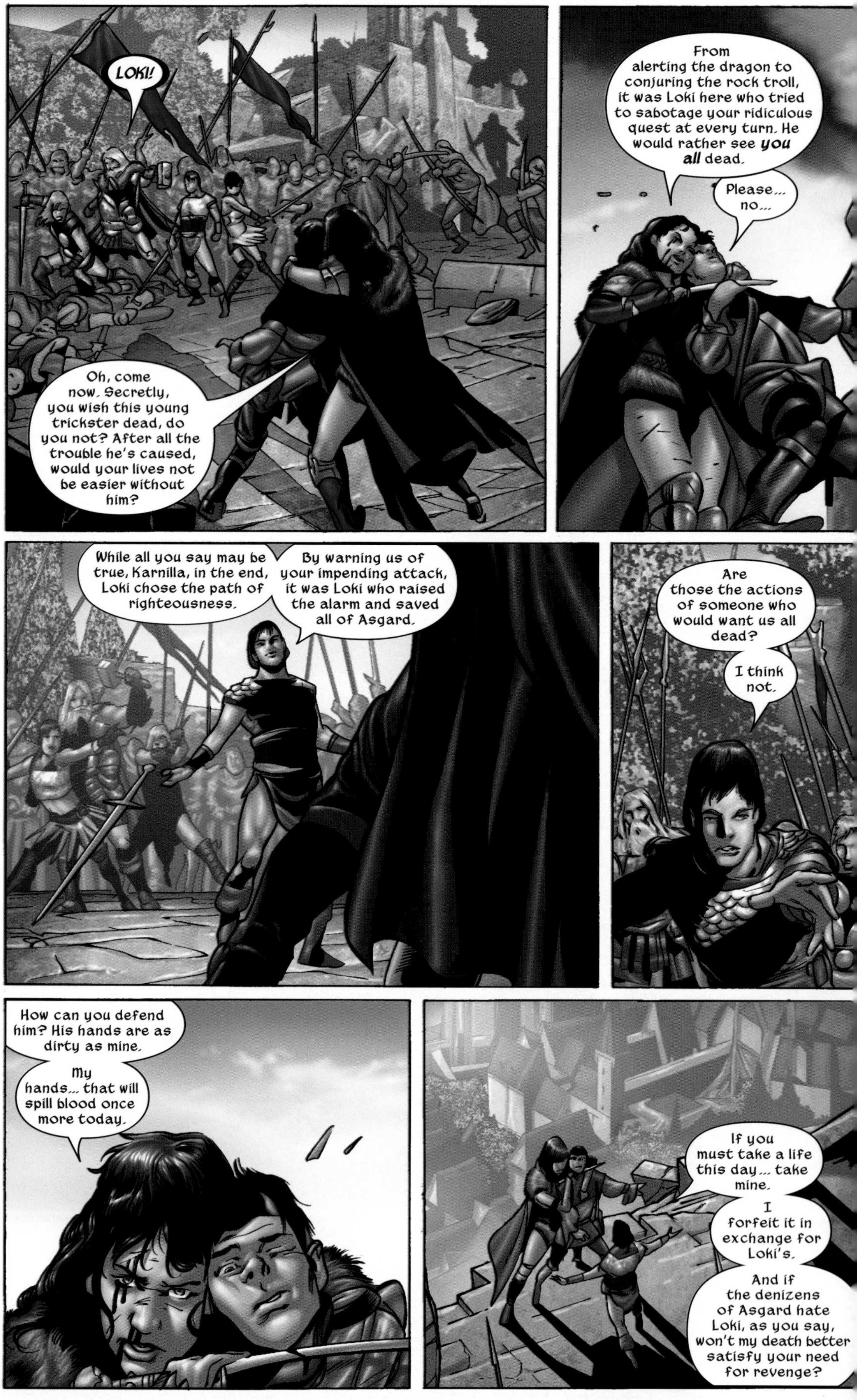
LOKI!
Oh, come now. Secretly, you wish this young trickster dead, do you not? After all the trouble he's caused, would your lives not be easier without him?
From alerting the dragon to conjuring the rock troll, it was Loki here who tried to sabotage your ridiculous quest at every turn. He would rather see *you all* dead.
Please... no...
While all you say may be true, Karnilla, in the end, Loki chose the path of righteousness.
By warning us of your impending attack, it was Loki who raised the alarm and saved all of Asgard.
Are those the actions of someone who would want us all dead?
I think not.
How can you defend him? His hands are as dirty as mine.
My hands... that will spill blood once more today.
If you must take a life this day... take mine.
I forfeit it in exchange for Loki's.
And if the denizens of Asgard hate Loki, as you say, won't my death better satisfy your need for revenge?

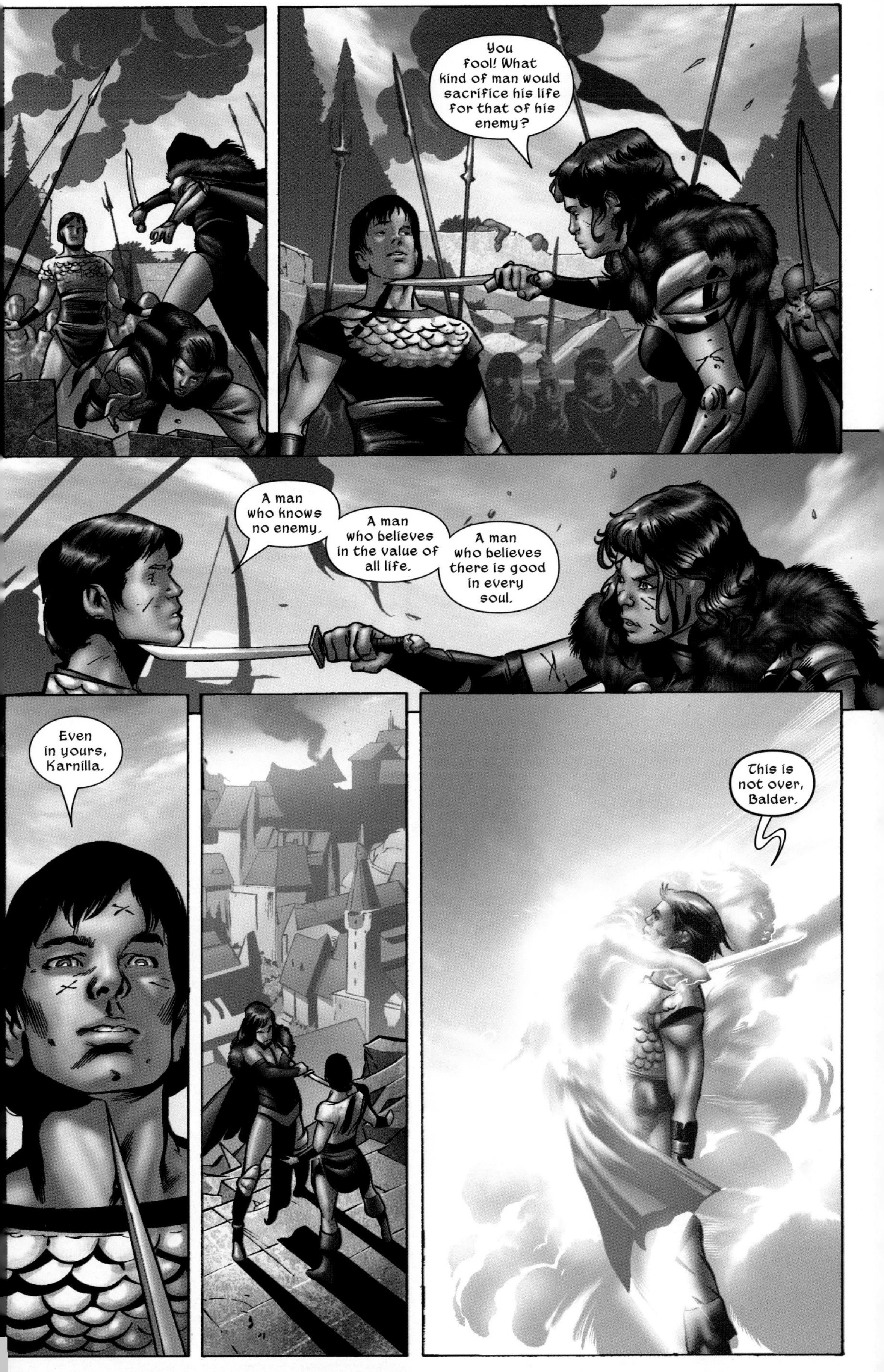
You fool! What kind of man would sacrifice his life for that of his enemy?
A man who knows no enemy.
A man who believes in the value of all life.
A man who believes there is good in every soul.
Even in yours, Karnilla.
This is not over, Balder.

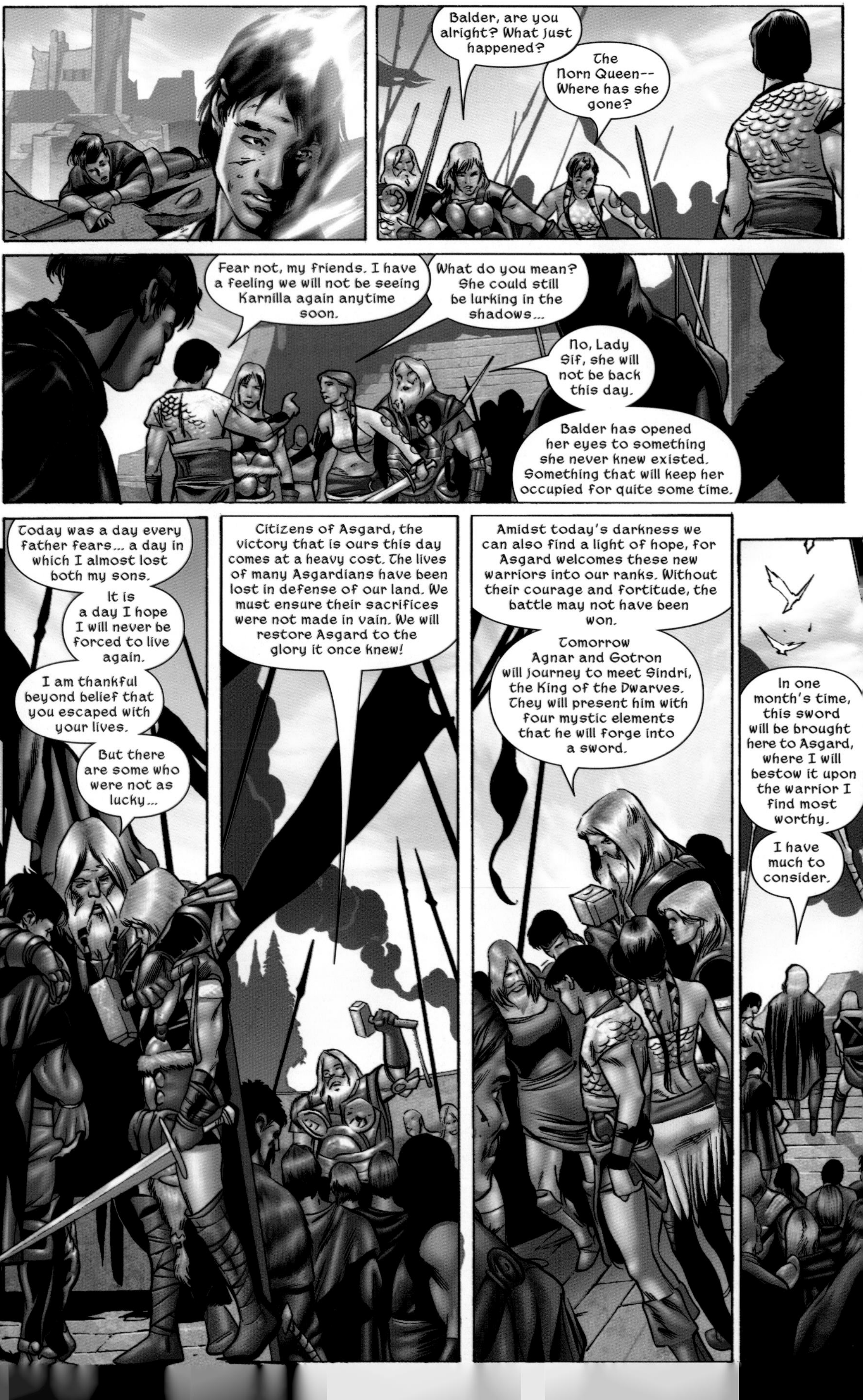
Balder, are you alright? What just happened?
The Norn Queen-- Where has she gone?
Fear not, my friends. I have a feeling we will not be seeing Karnilla again anytime soon.
What do you mean? She could still be lurking in the shadows...
No, Lady Sif, she will not be back this day.
Balder has opened her eyes to something she never knew existed. Something that will keep her occupied for quite some time.
Today was a day every father fears... a day in which I almost lost both my sons.
It is a day I hope I will never be forced to live again.
I am thankful beyond belief that you escaped with your lives.
But there are some who were not as lucky...
Citizens of Asgard, the victory that is ours this day comes at a heavy cost. The lives of many Asgardians have been lost in defense of our land. We must ensure their sacrifices were not made in vain. We will restore Asgard to the glory it once knew!
Amidst today's darkness we can also find a light of hope, for Asgard welcomes these new warriors into our ranks. Without their courage and fortitude, the battle may not have been won.
Tomorrow Agnar and Gotron will journey to meet Sindri, the King of the Dwarves. They will present him with four mystic elements that he will forge into a sword.
In one month's time, this sword will be brought here to Asgard, where I will bestow it upon the warrior I find most worthy.
I have much to consider.

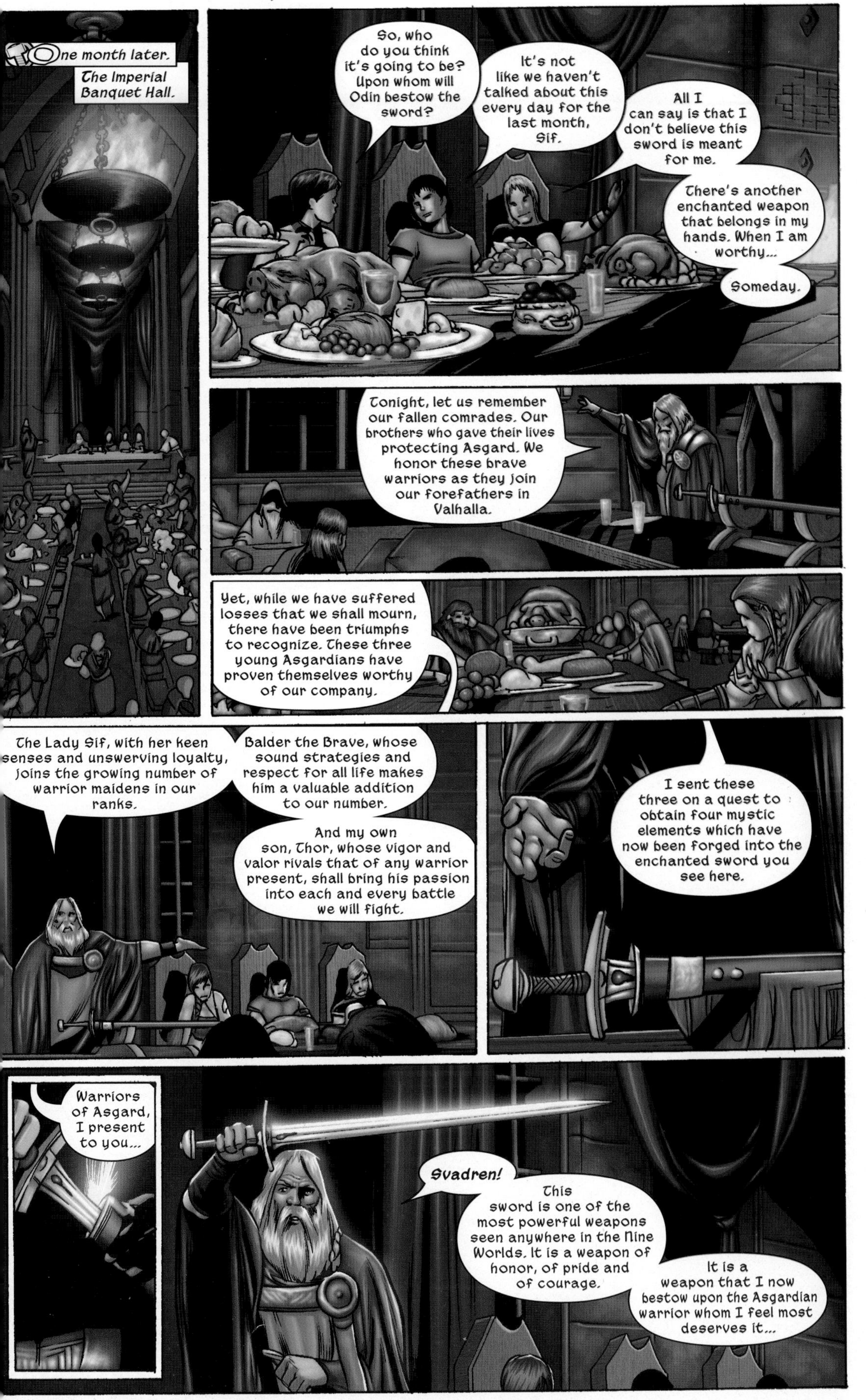
One month later.
The Imperial Banquet Hall.
So, who do you think it's going to be? Upon whom will Odin bestow the sword?
It's not like we haven't talked about this every day for the last month, Sif.
All I can say is that I don't believe this sword is meant for me.
There's another enchanted weapon that belongs in my hands. When I am worthy...
Someday.
Tonight, let us remember our fallen comrades. Our brothers who gave their lives protecting Asgard. We honor these brave warriors as they join our forefathers in Valhalla.
Yet, while we have suffered losses that we shall mourn, there have been triumphs to recognize. These three young Asgardians have proven themselves worthy of our company.
The Lady Sif, with her keen senses and unswerving loyalty, joins the growing number of warrior maidens in our ranks.
Balder the Brave, whose sound strategies and respect for all life makes him a valuable addition to our number.
And my own son, Thor, whose vigor and valor rivals that of any warrior present, shall bring his passion into each and every battle we will fight.
I sent these three on a quest to obtain four mystic elements which have now been forged into the enchanted sword you see here.
Warriors of Asgard, I present to you...
Svadren!
This sword is one of the most powerful weapons seen anywhere in the Nine Worlds. It is a weapon of honor, of pride and of courage.
It is a weapon that I now bestow upon the Asgardian warrior whom I feel most deserves it...

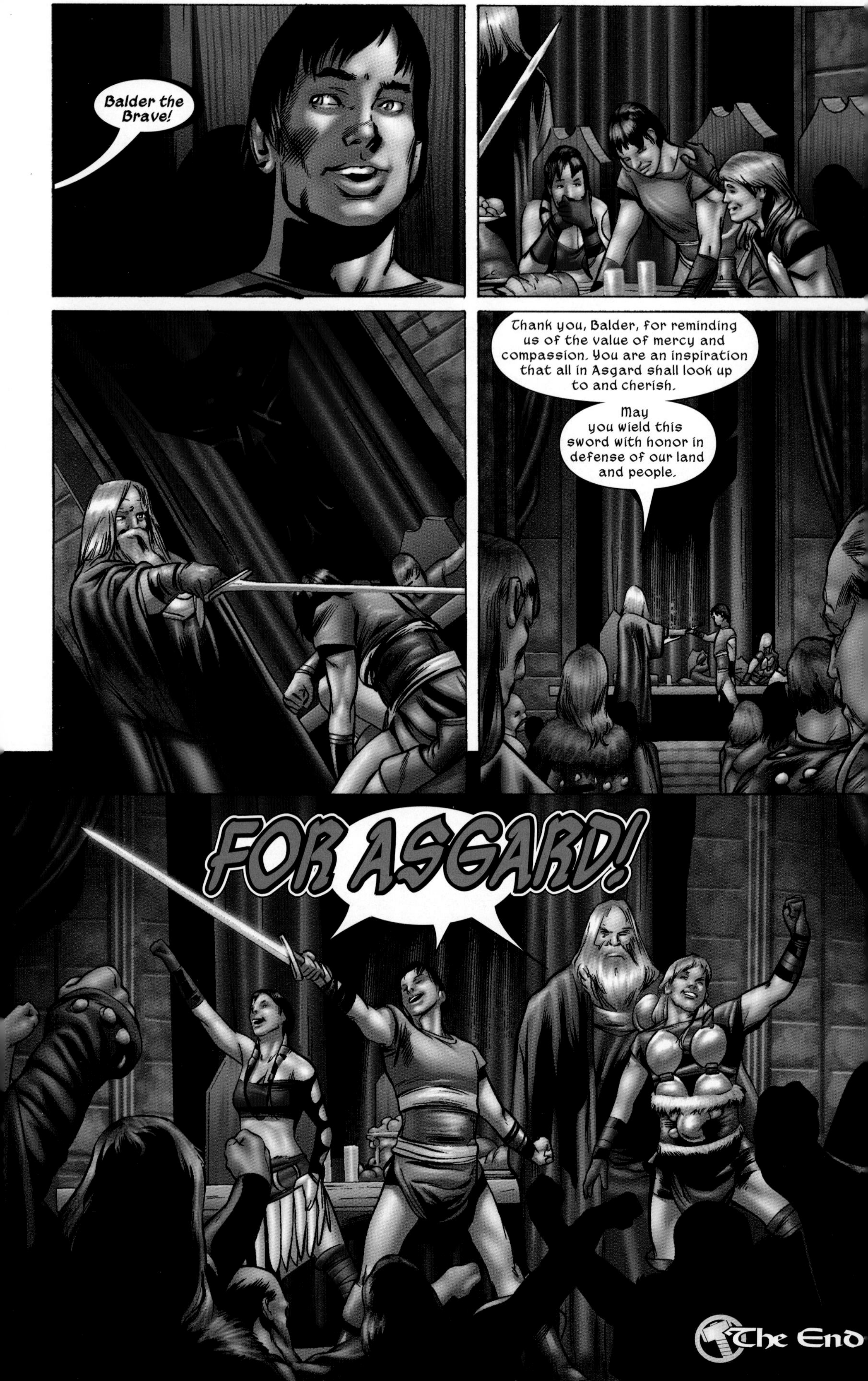
Balder the Brave!
Thank you, Balder, for reminding us of the value of mercy and compassion. You are an inspiration that all in Asgard shall look up to and cherish.
May you wield this sword with honor in defense of our land and people.
FOR ASGARD!
The End